The Bodyguards

SUSANTHA FERNANDO

Published by SUSANTHA FERNANDO, 2023.

This is a work of fiction. Similarities to real people, places, or events are entirely coincidental.

THE BODYGUARDS

First edition. April 8, 2023.

Copyright © 2023 SUSANTHA FERNANDO.

ISBN: 979-8215548004

Written by SUSANTHA FERNANDO.

This book is dedicated to Jean, Shereen and Shehan

THE BODYGUARDS

By Susantha Fernando

1. First day in the Café

It was a gloomy morning in West End, Glasgow. Locals walking in the rain through wet Ashton Lane, while tourists staring at them surprisingly. Jack was seated at his usual table at the English Breakfast, the first, next to the wide glass window near the entrance. That was the best place for the uninterrupted view. There are three tables along the wall either side. Four can sit at each conveniently. Two more small tables are outside in which two can accommodate.

Fresh flavors of coffee and toast smell moving swiftly in the warm air. This is Jack's usual breakfast stop. Some days he drops in to Willy's at corner towards Byres Road. But Willy's get crowded some mornings and seems restless and busy. Jack prefers a peaceful breakfast.

English Breakfast owner James, a brilliant man, running the whole place single handedly, with little support from his staff. He does not talk much, may be due to his busy schedule, but often polite and willing to listen to his customers eagerly. He is well aware of regulars, and their meal preferences.

The Carol brought in coffee with a smile.

"Here you are, breakfast will be here soon."

"Thank you Carol".

But Jack felt her smile is holding back a great sorrow. She was gazing through the wide window. It seems that she wanted to run away. Jack appreciates her politeness and the service very much. He wished to know her pain, so he could comfort her in some way. But they were not that close to discuss on such personal issues.

Suddenly, a gentleman walked in, opening the wide single door. Short but stout, removed his jacket tried to hang on the coat hanger but failed. Then again he threw it over and locked it with his brown hat. He walked up to the table opposite to Jack's and drop his leather brief case on it. Quickly he pulled the chair, sat, and pulled some papers out of his briefcase. He started on the papers as he has forgotten, he is in a café.

Carol approached him once he settled down.

"How may I help you sir?"

The gentlemen lifted his head briefly looked over his glasses and said "Coffee.........please".

"Anything you prefer sir? With milk or without? "

"With milk please" he did not lift his head.

"Single or double Expresso?" Carol asked again from the grumpy customer.

"Can I have a Cappuccino, please?"

He looked straight into Carol's eyes. Expression of his face gave a clear message, "Do not disturb me, anymore".

He immediately returned to his study or research ignoring all at the café.

Carol spend few minutes at the Expresso machine and returned with coffee. She served the coffee carefully to his left and placed the cup and sugar bowl on the table without any disturbance to the guest.

Later Carol brought Jack's daily breakfast, fried egg, sausages and toast bread. Jack do not order full English breakfast daily, which is expensive. James uses the quality products always for his café. Undoubtedly the full breakfast is the best in the street.

Jack opened the egg with the fork and let the egg yolk flow through the bread. He took butter and rubbed perfectly on toasted bread. The butter absorbed in to hot slices quickly. Jack looked at the guest at the table ahead. He seems upset, panic and restless. He scratched his head covered with half grey hair, then the forehead and looked through the window. While he returned to his documents, his eyes met Jack's. Jack stopped buttering and smiled at the guest. He looked surprised and returned to his documents again. Jack was embarrassed but wandered what upsets him so much.

Most of the customers walk into coffee shops and cafés are regulars. They know each other to certain extend unless if it is a tourist. It is a tradition here, even a newcomer get the same welcome as a regular. But

The English Breakfast's new guest seems preoccupied with something very important to his life.

He looked at the coffee, as if he just saw it lying there. He used two spoons of sugar, gazed on the cup for a while, and emptied the cup within few minutes.

"Bring the bill please" he requested carol.

Carol was by his side shortly with the bill. He put a pound note on the tray and waited impatiently for Carol's return. Carol brought back the balance and he took every coin on the tray carefully and put into his top pocket. He looked suddenly at his watch. He got impatient, walked swiftly to the coat hanger, put on his coat, bundle up all the documents ,pushed into his briefcase and walked swiftly back into the street.

Jack just finished his breakfast. He walked up to Carol, and gave her few coins extra for his breakfast and walked into the street. James and Carol both observing the new guest who is briskly walking towards the University Avenue. Jack turned to his right. He saw the new guest rushing down the lane and followed him few steps behind. He pulled a handkerchief to clean his nose and dropped something to the ground. He did not stop, but started moving quickly.

Jack found a visiting card which he dropped. It is from,

TERRY BLACKSTONE

ATTORNEY – AT – LAW

Jack ran behind him and tried to stop him. He saw Jack and stopped for a while.

"Sir...Sir..., I think you dropped this"

He put hand into his pocket to search something and approached Jack with a smile.

"Or thank you very much Mr., I have a meeting with this gentlemen within few minutes. I would have been in a big mess without this business card. So thank you very much again."

"That's Ok." Jack replied.

Looking at the business card Jack told, "This is not that far, just few blocks toward your left down the University Avenue"

"Thank you Mr., I need to go now will meet up later" He stopped further discussions with Jack.

Jack nodded and watched him moving towards the building. He stopped and looked at a sand stone old building, checked the business card jack just returned to him, and vanished into the building.

Jack was happy with the morning incident, that he could help the grumpy gentlemen and to see a smile on his face, before a sour memory recorded in his mind. Jack wished to meet him again somewhere in the city. He was eager to know why he was so upset. But he never knew this stranger would change his life upside down.

Jack came back to earth and suddenly realized he is getting late to office. He crossed the street and walked toward to his office.

2. Disappearance

Jack joined Jenny's News Daily, three years ago. He started his journalism career in his home town Airdrie, with a local online newspaper. Nigel, the editor trained him and pushed hard to get the best out of him.

"Jack, once you have some news, go deeper and find out everything in all angles. Don't be scared, we need to take risk when it is necessary to find info. You are a talented young man. Keep pushing, ask questions, to get the best for news". This was Nigel's one of the daily lectures.

But Nigel could not push that far, one day, just after Christmas holidays, he had a heart attack. He died suddenly before they took him to the hospital.

Sub- Editor took over the newspaper, but Jack was not the kind of journalist the new editor needed. Jack left for Glasgow hoping to get a job for survival. He did two or three part- time jobs per day until he got into Jenny's as a journalist. Jack handles everything, including camera, presentation, interviewing and editing. It was tough at the beginning to adjust into complete complex context as a journalist. But Jenny's patients made Jack a useful hand for the newspaper.

Jack walked in to the editorial meeting one morning. They have two meetings, morning 9.00 and evening 4.00. The discussions helped mainly to ensure they have sufficient contents for the day and how those support the values of the newspaper. Jenny has started the meeting already when Jack walked in and he sat next to Paul. Paul covers issues dealing with law enforcement. He has insiders to get confidential information and documents.

Jenny a former main stream media sub-editor has 30 years of experience in the field with useful network including number of important political figures. These secret information boosted Jeanie's daily views past fifty thousand.

Jack covers social issues, such as high prices, housing, healthcare and many more. But he loved the Paul's subject very much. But he did not have the network and the experience required to support the newspaper same as Paul did. But Paul as a friend, sometimes invited Jack also for his field work.

At the last stages of the meeting,

"Jack, get some interviews on week to week consumer prices. I know there is a noticeable increase. Try to cover all parties concern" Jenny said.

"I have two cases I cover, have some updates which are interesting turning points. So I think that would do for today" Paul looked at Jenny expecting her feedback.

Jenny asked "Anything new Paul?"

"Well I got an information of a missing person, not from here. But the complaint lodged by his family and the hotel he stayed. I got the photo as well" Paul pull out a printout of a middle aged man and turn the paper towards Jenny.

Jenny seems curios and told "Try to get something for this today Paul. This will be interesting"

"Fine I'll try my best" and Paul took the paper back from Jenny, but Jack took the paper from him for a closer look.

It was the stranger at the English Breakfast, who Jack met couple of days ago.

"Do you know this guy, Jack?" Paul asked.

But something within told Jack to be silent.

"Hmm... not ah really. But he looks like one of my relatives, but this is not him." Jack lied.

"Do you know his name. " Jack asked.

"He is William Selwyn, an estate broker, from Hale, Manchester." Paul replied.

Jack tried to recall his memories of William, while Jenny wrapped up the meeting shortly afterwards.

Jack walked to his desk thinking of missing William. He did not have much time to ponder, but to be back on the street quickly for his task of the day. His back pack weighed on his right shoulder. He moved towards the city center. He sat on a bench near a café, fixed his smart phone to the rig, a mike and fixed his ear phone as well. Then he took his small note book from the top pocket of his backpack wrote few points on the questions to ask from consumers.

He walked up to a supermarket, waited outside to talk to few citizens who were leaving with their purchases.

Jack moved into an elderly gentlemen and asked few questions.

"Look young man, I am a pensioner. My pension increases with inflation. But the prices doesn't match with the inflation that they say. Heating prices doubled last year, I barely manage to survive last winter. Now they're going to increase again. How me and my wife going to survive? Don't they have any understanding how people are suffering in this country?

"I'll tell you, they are not bothered. They just want to squeeze everything we have and fill rich people's pockets. I am disgusted of our leaders and Westminster."

Jack was walking person to person and he got nothing but negative and hopeless comments of their future. He filled with dark deep feeling. He called Cabinet Secretary's office for a quick meeting with the secretary. But she was not available. Her office staff did not want to comment for any issues Jack laid down.

He came to office and started compiling bits and pieces of his article with video clips. He went through the recent news updates and publications of Cabinet Secretaries office find suitable clips for his article. However he fixed a meeting with Cabinet Secretary on following Tuesday. Jack uploaded the article after the evening editorial meeting.

He went back to English Breakfast in the evening for cup of tea with some James delicious cookies. He waited patiently to see if James will initiate the discussion of William. But he was silent.

"Hey James, heard that guy gone missing" Jack told James.

James seems surprised and replied "which guy Jack?"

James knew everything happening in Glasgow. He was silent, but well connected man. He gets all the information of the city on his table, within days. Jack was surprised how he did not know.

"The guy who came here suddenly and had a coffee at that table" Jack pointed the table opposite to him.

"Jack frankly speaking I cannot remember tourist who walked in here once but may be after few visits here, yes" James replied.

"But I'll tell you one thing. If someone goes missing in Glasgow means, it is not an accident. It is for a reason. You and I should not know the people involved. Because they can be dangerous. And for them Police always be silent or do soft paddling. So my advice Jack, stay away." James voice was stern, had a serious tone of warning.

Jack did not talk about William again in the Café. He knew James do not like the subject.

But as a journalist he cannot just be silent. He remembered Nigel's advice. "Take the risk and find all info".

So he decided to take the risk.

3. Investigation

Jack allocated one hour of his time daily for the investigation on William. This is what he loved to do. But for some reason, he decided not to inform Paul or Jenny regarding this investigation.

Next day, after his daily newspaper routine, he took time off to go through all possible articles in that day or in archive on disappearance of Mr. William. Jack could not find much except a brief description of William and his business in Glasgow. He checked William's information on the internet. But could not find anything interesting except brief LinkedIn page as an Estate Broker.

He was a licensed surveyor and valuer of Royal Institute of Chartered Surveyors (RICS). There were interesting properties he was involved mainly in Manchester. Now then what? Jack thought. He decided to start form the building he walked into. Then he remembered the business card. "Terry Blackstone".

Then he searched information on Terry. As on the internet, Mr. Terry Blackstone is a business lawyer and investor. He is an influential shareholder of a ship building facility down the river Clyde. And owner of many small companies including real estate and investment banking. Jack could not find much on Terry as a practicing a lawyer. He was a lawyer of Anderson's and became a partner of another law firm and then seems running a private practice down University Avenue. Probably the building Williams walked into. Jack decided to walk down the University Avenue and observe the building from distance.

It was red stone building with white framed windows. Jack was looking for an evidence of Terry's office in that. He walk up to the building, walked up few steps to the main entrance and found Terry's office's name board, "Terry Blackstone – Attorney at Law". He did not have any excuse to go into Terry's office.

Jack reluctantly walked back few steps down to find a homeless man sitting, looking at the street. He has covered his whole top with old brown jacket with the hood. He was just about to pass the man and he recognized him. He was John. A homeless man, who did a part in his video on the homeless issue, in Glasgow few months ago.

"Hi John!" Jack called him. He was trying to identify Jack, but seems unknown. But as a homeless man he smiles with anyone, as he had to depend on someone for his next meal. Jack bend down in front of him to show his face clearly, can you remember our program we did for Jenny's news daily?

"Oh", John remembered. "Nothing happened afterwards, we are still here." John complained.

Jack had a deep breath and said "we did what we can do John. Our article and videos send a message to relevant authorities, city council, and even cabinet secretary. But their response is slow and poor. But we will do this continuously."

"That's fine, I know that very well. But what brought you here? You came to meet Terry?" John asked.

Jack replied "not exactly."

"I'll tell you my friend, don't hire him as a lawyer. He could be the shrewdest man you are going to deal with. I sit close to this building most of the time and Terry is the only one staying here. I watched him and his clients. I get the information from my underground buddies. He is a dangerous man, be careful."

Jack was taken back by his comment and thought of getting more information of Terry.

"Shall we get some coffee for us, John? Come on." Jack walked down the University Street with John searching the nearest café. He had no idea he is walking into a danger.

4. The Body Guards

Jack and John walked down University Avenue little further. Jack bought two cups of coffee and crossed the lane. They sat on a long concrete bench started sipping their coffee leisurely.

"What brought you to Terry, Jack?" John inquired.

"Did you hear about a missing man in Glasgow recently?" Jack questioned John.

"Why not. I don't read newspapers, but I get all city gossip up to date" John smiled at Jack.

"That guy is William right?" John asked from Jack.

"Yes, he is one of my distance relative. What else you know about him John?" Jack asked again.

"Oh dear! I didn't know that. I am so sorry to hear that." John seems worried and upset.

"I need to tell you something that might be very painful for you. He will not come back." John ended with sigh.

"What? How do you know that? Have you seen someone kidnapping him? Oh did you see William anyway? Jack's questioning stopped at that point. He was staring at John.

But John was sipping his coffee slowly looking down on the tile work of the pavement. He did not talk for few minutes.

Then he told Jack, "My friend I am 66 years old now. I spend all of my life in Glasgow. I know the heartbeat of this city very well."

John Continued," Do you know how many disappeared in this city? I can give you so many names? They disappeared. For some, after a long investigation, found their bodies. But never.....never....... never found the murderer." John said without lifting his head to Jack.

Jack thought, John might be comparing few incidents without investigating with details. But then, John looked at Jack and asked. "Do you know why Jack? These crimes are executed by the city Elite and

Scotland Yard is either soft-peddling or faking the evidence to protect the murderer, for a big pay check"

John continued, "You know Jack, Scotland Yard solves almost 90% of their cases. But 10% of those they do not solve, are related to organized crimes. This is where they get big money. So, now few days passed. If it is an ordinary case, we would have find a clue where his body or place where they have murdered him. But don't get upset Jack. I am guessing, with my experience, he is gone."

Jack had a very unpleasant feeling, a pain that he cannot explain. Jack do not like to tolerate injustice. Even William is not his relative, he wanted to know what happened to him. According to John, even with Jack's own experiences, sometime Police do not work as a law enforcement office, but unjustly enforcing the law against innocent and helpless ordinary people.

John realized Jack is very upset of the incident while he was gazing down the University Avenue. He tapped Jack's shoulder and got up and told "Jack don't worry I get some information of William by tomorrow afternoon. You come here tomorrow after office, good bye for now."

Jack watched John walking down the road. He watched him until he disappeared among the people. Then he got up and walked back to his office. He reached office but no one seems to be in except Jenny. Jack took his bag came back to the street, expecting to walk slowly to his room.

While he was walking, a boy quickly came near him on a bicycle and gave him a small white envelope and got away quickly. He was dressed with grey track bottom and white jacket with a hood. Jack could not grasp his face as it was covered with the hood. Jack did not know what to do with the letter. But decided to walk back to office and open the letter.

He was at his table within minutes. He held the letter against the light to see what could be inside. It appears to him a small folded paper. He cautiously opened the letter. It was a small paper 4" by 4". Typed and printed, seems cut into four by four. No address or date. Just one sentence and a name below. Letter stated,

STAY AWAY FROM WILLIAM'S AFFAIRS.
BODYGUARDS.

Jack was puzzled. Is this a threat? Who is "Bodyguards"? He wanted to call Paul, but Jack did not trust Paul much as he acted sometimes in a suspicious ways. Jack walked towards Jenny's office taped on the door.

Jenny smiled and said "come in Jack. Why you are still here?"

"I just left office for my room, but on the way I got this. Can you get something out of it?" Jack asked.

Jenny took the small letter read carefully. "Oh! My God" Jenny exclaimed.

"You saw who gave this?" Jenny asked. "Teenager I think, could not see his face, was covered with his Jacket hood." Jack replied.

"William is the guy who disappeared few days ago, right?" Jenny questioned again. "Do you have anything to do with him, Jack?" Jenny leaned back and looked at Jack expecting an answer.

Jack paused for a while, and said "Well, William came to English Breakfast last Monday morning. I left the café just after he left and was walking behind him down the University Avenue. I helped him to get his dropped visiting card of Terry Blackstone, the lawyer. He thanked me and told me he is going to meet Terry. Then this Wednesday we got to know he has disappeared. So William met Terry before his disappearance."

"Wow, that's it?" Jenny was curious.

"No, then this afternoon I went near Terry's office." Jack confessed. "But I did not go in, but then I met John. Can you remember John who joined for the 'Glasgow Homeless Speaks' program?"

"Yes, I can" Jenny nodded. "I met him at the entrance of Terry's office. I had a long chat with him. He was pessimistic of William's return" Jack stopped for a while and asked "Who are these Bodyguard's?

"Well Jack" Jenny sighed again, "They are one of the strongest gangs who are mainly controlling the West – End."

"Jack, now they know you are behind this story. Not only that, they are watching every move you make. These guys are brutal murderers. Be careful now." Jenny warned Jack.

"Why are you so interested of this issue? Paul is working on this right?" Jenny asked again.

"I don't know. I met him only once in my lifetime. Shared few words with him. Now I know he is not there. I thought I was curious at first." Jack added.

"But now I have a doubt whether justice will ever been served for William. So now I am seeking justice for him." And Jack continued, "True, I know this is not my area. I will give this information to Paul Jenny."

"No, don't do that. " Jenny said, "Don't ever tell this to Paul."

"Why?" Jack wondered.

"Don't asked me now Jack. I cannot tell you. But it is safer not to inform Paul for now." Jenny looked at the piece paper again and gave it to Jack.

"If you are confident you can get more information on this. But be very careful not to expose yourself to anyone too much. Do it secretly. Give me an update daily. I will tell you when to run this story. If you get into trouble call me immediately at any time. I will help you." Jenny smiled again.

"Thank you Jack then, I need to go home now." Jenny got up.

"Thank you Jenny" Jack walked out from Jenny's office.

5. Evidence

Next day evening, after a hard day's work, Jack did not forget John. He bought Coffee for both. Jack walked up to the benches where he and John met yesterday afternoon down the University Avenue. Jack could not find John anywhere near. He sat on one of those empty concrete benches expecting John to show up. John came walking after few minutes later. He did not look at him, his eyes focused towards the opposite direction of the road. He came closer to John and was passing him completely ignoring Jack's presence. But John whispered Jack "come into the mall."

Jack gave john few minutes and grab the coffee and walked in to the mall. Jack did not see John in the mall. He passed few display units and few shops. But he was gone. Jack thought of walking back out of the mall. While he was turning a rough hand pulled him into a small shop. It was John. He guided Jack to back of the shop.

John spoke softly. He had fear in his eyes and his words did not flow smoothly as it was yesterday.

"I ah….I have some information for you Jack" John finally uttered.

"William and Terry had left Terry's office around 11.00 a.m. yesterday. You know where they were afterwards? At English breakfast. No one has seen William leaving the Café. But Alex left the café, by 1.00 p.m." John concluded.

"Why they do not give this information to Police? This is crucial for the investigation right?" Jack exclaimed.

John gestured Jack to be silent. "They know the guys behind this incident are so powerful. Then, no point telling police about it. Nothing will happen," John added.

John spoke again softly "someone is watching you Jack. Yesterday I went down to city center to meet a guy to get this information. It was late evening. When I returned, one guy bumped into me. He seems to me a gangster. A young guy. He asked me "what do you have to do with Jack?"

John continued, "I was shocked how he got your name. But I try to pacify his anger saying about your connection with me during the program. But he did not take any notice."

"Then he said, 'stay away from him, let him do his own investigations. If you talk to him again, you will die like a dog down the parking lot.' Then he pushed me to a side and vanished into the darkness." John sighed.

"Sorry Jack, I don't think I can help you any more, or come to you with any information. You are on your own now." John paused and said "But if I get anything important, I'll try to pass on to you somehow."

"Thanks John, but don't take that risk." Jack told John. "But why you guys say that Police will not do anything" Jack asked again.

John replied "This morning Police took their K9s down the road for William's investigation. May be to find some evidence on him. But they never took dogs down Ashton lane. Why they did that Jack?" John continued "Because they are avoiding important evidence for someone. Now do you get how these things work here in Scotland?"

John held Jack's shoulders and said "Jack you are a good man. I would like to help you. But take courage and continue carefully, get whatever information you need. Begin your investigation form English breakfast."

Jack realized that he is holding two cups of coffee in his hand. He gave both to John and turned back to leave the mall. "Both for me?" John asked.

"Yeah, I am not in a mood now, bye." Jack left the mall into the darkness.

Jack decided to go to his favorite café next morning, the English breakfast. Jack cannot talk about William there, but just needed to sit and observe anything suspicious. But in his situation, he might see both James and Carol suspicious. But he decided to go anyway. He did not know the shocking experience awaiting for him next day.

6. English Breakfast

Jack reached English Breakfast in the morning. Jack was first to walk-in. James and Carol seems surprised to see Jack in the Café. He did not get usual well come. Jack said good morning first, while they were staring at each other. Jack felt that they did not want Jack to be at the Café that morning. However, he got his breakfast followed by his coffee. Jack purposely took longer to finish his breakfast, expecting a suspicious act in the café.

Then Jack thought all this incidence could be created by his suspicious mind. They may have nothing to do with William. The information he received was from unreliable and unverified sources. How James and Carol could commit such a crime in the midday in Glasgow? Jack smiled for his own immaturity and took the fork to finish his breakfast soon.

Street garbage collectors walking down the lane collecting garbage bins. Carol looked at James and he nodded. Carol walked through the "staff only" door behind the counter. After few minutes Carol brought a bin, seems to be a food waste. She was holding the bin with one hand but never called any of the collectors, those passing by the café, collecting bins placed for disposal. One grey haired middle aged collector came and he took the bin. Why Carol has to bring the bin outside? Bin collectors do it by themselves.

Jack then noticed James had been watching him over the counter. He smiled at Jack. It was faked smile obviously. Jack felt very uncomfortable when he saw Carol also was watching at him while entering cafés back yard entrance. Jack left cash on the table for the food and left abruptly as he felt uneasy to stay there any further.

He walked back to the office, while pondering on the incidents happened in the café. He had some work again in the streets today, but he lost his mood without any clear reason. While he was walking down the Byres road he heard announcement in community center and noted a gathering in the center. While he was passing he heard, "please welcome Mr. Terry Blackstone." Jack stopped on the spot. He pulled out his note book, ran across the street and got inside the center.

He had to present his journalist ID to go closer to the speaker. There were many journalist known to Jack, seated in the front. He was standing in the corner and eagerly listening to him. Jack scrutinized features of Terry inch by inch. His hair was shaved with number one, sharp dark eyes, thick eye browses, straight sharp nose, and both corners of lips turning downward indicating he cannot smile without a great effort. He was dressed with black suit and a black tie that suits a lawyer.

Minister of business seems just finished his speech. He was talking to few officials on the platform.

Terry was speaking,

"........So as I explained, this program is introducing today, to encourage all SME sector entrepreneurs, so it will assist all members of this organization to stand strong again with government support, to overcome challenges of post-Covid period. I Thank you honorable minister your presence today to initiate this program and we look forward for your continuous support and contribution for Glasgow SME community."

And then a round of applause.....

Journalist questioned Terry, indicating that he should be the leader of SME community in Glasgow. Jack was listening to all those boring meaningless questions until his turn comes. After few minutes Terry pointed to Jack.

Jack was not ready, all ordinary questioned covered by other journalists. But then something within Jack raised a question for Terry.

"Yes, a......just an ordinary question" Jack said. ""One Mr. William, had been disappeared few days ago in this area West-End. What is your view of that incident?"

It was Obvious, Terry stunned by Jack's question. The Minister also seems a bit uncomfortable. He also looked straight at Jack. Terry's strong features tuned from shocked to Anger.

"You are from where?" Terry rudely asked Jack to buy time for the answer.

Jack showed his ID."I am Jack, from "Jenny's daily."

"Oh, Paul's newspaper." Terry murmured. "How this is related to this forum" Terry growled.

Jack was shocked that he knew Paul. Paul never mentioned about Terry with Jack before. Jack thought of an excuse. "Well it is important for any investor to have a reliable law enforcement system in the region for a safe investment. So as a leader of this organization, how you look at this incident. Will this delay of justice is good for businesses?" Jack found some words to cover up.

Jack didn't know why he asked such a silly a question. Now he is struggling to come out of it. Terry's anger still glowing in his face.

Minister intervene "Well... gentleman, we are well aware of this incident and our law enforcement officers are working round the clock to find all suspects soon. We have our trust in them. They are already have some clues. We believe very soon, we will get to know the truth. I always wish that there is no harm happened to Mr. William."

The meeting concluded afterward. There were some hand shaking among the guests and audience. Jack started walking out of the community hall and glanced back at the stage. Then he saw Terry and the minister staring at him and discussing something seriously. Jack blamed himself for his foolishness. He revealed himself to the probable enemies. But Jack cannot still understand why he asked that question. But he was just heading for another mess.

7. Another Gang?

Jack walk back to the office and thought of writing a small note on the conference for tomorrow's upload. Jack got a cup of coffee and was busy keying the article on his desktop. Then couple messages popped up on his phone. Jack ignored first, but continuous buzzing disturbed him. He took the phone and there were few messages.

"Are you in office?"

"Need to meet you."

"It is urgent, need to meet you now"

"Can I come in to your office?"

"It is better if I can meet you now"

Jack thought this must be someone who wanted him to do an article.

Jack checked the number, but it was an undisclosed number. That was suspicious. He was scared and anxious. While he was wandering what to do, someone pressed the doorbell. As there was no one in the office, Jack had to open the door. He was in fear. He walked up to the door and looked at the CCTV camera monitor and saw a well-dressed gentlemen standing near the door. He suppressed his thought with great effort and bravely opened the door expecting a gun, pointed to his forehead.

But there was polite smiling gentlemen instead.

"Are you Jack?" he asked with his uninterrupted smile.

"Yes I am" Jack nodded.

"I just messaged you can I talked to you for few minutes? Sorry for the intrusion. But it is very, very, urgent."

Jack did not know what to say. "Ok then come in." Jack invited the guest into the office. He guided him into the meeting room and directed him to sit and then Jack sat on the chair in front the guest.

"Yes, what is this all about?" Jack asked the visitor.

"Well I know you hold some important information regarding Mr. William, as per the information I have." The guest described the purpose of his visit.

Jack was shocked and did not know what to say. "May I know your name please? And you're from?" Jack asked quickly form the stranger.

"Well Jack, I would like to keep those blank for the moment until we have some agreement." He replied.

"If you want to know my background, I represent an organization opposing 'Bodyguards'. Do you know about them?" He asked Jack.

"I am not that sure of that" Jack said. But the stranger smiled back awkwardly.

"You know who Bodyguards are Jack. You already met them." He stopped smiling anymore.

Jack replied out of fear whisperingly, "I am not sure what you are talking about." He was determine not to talk about the threat letter he received from 'Bodyguards'.

The stranger responded again.

"Jack, you have all your reasons to suspect me. I do understand. But let me explain to you what's happening out there.

'Bodyguards' are not a small criminal organization. It is well established in whole UK. But they control certain areas in each county, Northern Ireland, Wales and here in Scotland. We are strong in Scotland. We do not have full control of Glasgow, especially West-End."

"Control for what?" Jack interrupted.

"You know Jack, all black businesses handled by Criminal groups? Even drugs." Stranger continued.

"So let me continue. As I said the Bodyguard's control West-End. The big boss of Bodyguard's is Terry. He controls everything here in Glasgow. And your favorite breakfast spot, English Breakfast, is the center for drug distribution in West-End. James handles it. Carol also involve in it. Every supplier of English Breakfast is a Bodyguard. Guy who brought the letter to you is the legal clerk of Terry. He is Kevin. They are just trainees of Bodyguard's. They distribute stuff, information, and letters and sometime get involve in minor street fights, but of course with a supervisor."

Jack could not believe what he was listening.

The stranger spoke again "the information that you are holding is vital, to take down Terry. I am a professional who supports the criminals opposing 'Bodyguards. We cannot expect justice in Scotland, through the law enforcement system. Because it is corrupted to the extremes. What we can do is support similar opposing powers to control your enemy. Terry has their guys in Police and we also have people that we can get things done. We can send K9s to English Breakfast and nail Terry and Bodyguard network here in Glasgow. "

"Terry is your enemy?" Jack asked.

"Not only him, the whole organization. It is a long story I do not want to waste your time. But I do not involve in operational work of the gang that I support. I assist them on professional matters." he replied.

But Jack was still wandering. Is it a trick of the same people to get all information from him? But he did not want to share anything yet.

The stranger sighed. "Jack you are in a great danger. You do not know how long you live because they are watching you. The question you asked at the community center was really unnecessary. Now they will expedite their plans on you. Police cannot protect you. But we can protect you. Let me know once change your mind. You can reply the messages I send. Then I will get it. Thank you for your time Jack. Have a nice and safe evening. Good night." Stranger got up and left the office swiftly.

Jack spend some time in the meeting room. He now know he is in a deep trouble. But how he can get out of it? He wanted to share this with Jenny as soon as possible. But he did not want to tell this on the phone. He do not know whether his phone also is tapped already. But his troubles were not yet over.

8. The Murder

Jack walked in to the street and started walking aimlessly. People were busy in their own worlds. Some university students were walking in the opposite side of the street, laughing and mocking at each other. Are they very happy? Why I cannot be happy like them? He regretted involving in William's matters. William was a total stranger and now he has become Jack's whole life purpose. His life and death is in the balance now, as a result of investigating on William's murder.

Then suddenly someone knock on his right shoulder bit harder. Jack was annoyed. Why, he has so much of room here, is he blind? The guy whispered. "Jack I am John. Follow me to the mall after a while." Then John moved on.

Jack kept walking in the same direction for a while avoid any suspicious. Then he walked in to the closest café and ordered a coffee. "On the double miss" Jack smiled at the barista. He smiled after many days he realized. The girl was preparing the coffee very fast and smiled back at Jack. Coffee was ready instantly. Jack was just about to walk out of the café and barista said "take the bill sir."

"No that's Ok" Jack tried to walk out, but she wrote something behind the bill and forcefully gave to Jack, and she told "read the other side later." Jack smiled and put the bill in his jacket pocket. He thought that must be her number. Jack smiled again and felt his left cheek and thought, it's good to have someone with all this trouble, a girl friend. Jack had been not dating since he came to Glasgow. He walked into the mall and wandered for John. He stopped for a while and pulled the bill out and read. It was not a number.

"A Bodyguard is following you. Be careful" Jack could not move further. He was scared to look around thinking the spy could be watching him. Jack gathered some strength and turned towards a corridor of stalls and then John pulled him into a stall and grabbed his hand took him into a small store room, back of the stall and closed the door. Jack's coffee almost spilled during this hasty move. There were two small stools inside and John sat on one showing the other to Jack. He sat without a word. John removed the hood of the jacket. The dim light of the room did not highlight the fear in their faces clearly.

Then Jack showed the note on the bill. John struggled a bit to read it with the dim light.

John said "Oh my God,......... my G...o...d. But they will not come into this mall. This belongs to another gang. So don't worry in here. But they can spy on you."

"I have a terrifying news for you Jack" John continued. "I do not know how to say this."

Jack said, "I am terrified already, so go ahead."

"William was murdered inside the 'English Breakfast' on the same day he visited there with Terry."

"What?" Jack was shocked. "How they did that, in midday at the center of the city?"

John smiled and said, "They are gangsters, they can do anything, anywhere." He paused for a sigh, and continued. "They have cut his body in to small pieces and mixed with other disposals and given to the waste disposal company. The company has dumped them in to a landfill. But not exactly at the land fill but further into the jungle."

Then Jack asked, "Do you have strong witnesses for this murder John."

"Yes I have" John said.

"Then why you people do not come forward and inform police?" Jack angrily asked John.

"I told you before Jack, no point, nothing will happen." John pause for a while and continued.

"But if someone can get a professional lawyer and guide us in this case, I can ask them to come forward. If you are interested you can lead us Jack."

Jack knows exactly, the consequence of leading a team of witnesses against a criminal gang. He felt the fear of torture and death. But he did not say anything.

"Ok Jack I have to leave now, let me know if you are going do something about it. Be careful." John concluded the discussion, opened the door and left the stall. Jack followed him little later.

9. Guilt and Justice

Jack safely reached his apartment. He wandered whether to call Jenny and inform events of the day. Community center gathering, strangers visit and the eye witnesses he has.

Finally he called Jenny. "Evening Jenny, it was a hectic day today. I have some information of William."

"I'll call you back, give me few minutes." She cut the line.

After few moments Jack got a call from an undisclosed number. First he thought this could be the stranger who visited him today. He did not answer immediately, but as the person was not willing to give up Jack answered the call. It was Jenny.

She told" Sorry Jack, I don't think it is good to discuss on my phone on this matter. So what happened Jack?"

Jack explained everything from confrontation of Terry to John's information in detail.

"John is willing to bring the witnesses if I lead this case. Let me know what to do Jenny."

Jenny replied "as John said, there will be no justice for William. We can run an article about this incident. But first you have to meet all his witnesses personally and ensure these evidence are reliable. We have to do this in extremely confidential manner."

She continued "I'll tell you Jack, I have reliable evidence that Paul also a Bodyguard. So be careful that he should not know anything."

"Oh my God" Jack cried. "I was sitting next to a dangerous man. Terry seems to be knowing him well. He told me that at the gathering today."

"Yes that is possible" Jenny continued" The first, you decide whether you are willing to take the risk. Once we publish this article, Police will ask me to come forward with the evidence. It is good to keep journalist name anonymous. So we can tell we will present the witnesses at the courts. But I have to take a deadly risk for this. So Jack first you decide and bring me those reliable evidence. The meeting place for this article should not be in our office. I suggest it should be out of the city probably in a vehicle. But you have to make the decision first. Think carefully and let me know tomorrow. Good night Jack" Jenny disconnected the call.

After dinner Jack tried his best to evaluate the consequences, comparing the risk and the justice. He was just stepping in to an investigative journalism. Hopefully John trusts him. But will john's informants trust him as well? What kind of group that they belong to? How dangerous these groups could be? Then Jack might need protection from both witness and the suspect. Is this risk necessary? Is he capable of handling this serious mission? A question after another.

Jack tried to sleep and forget completely all incidents from the day he first met William to date. But he could not sleep a bit. As much as he tried to forget, all incidents popped up one after the other, as he was watching a murder movie. Why I cannot forget William? He is no one of mine. He is not from here and not from his town Airdrie. Why then?

It is not my area. That is Paul's. Why I have to work on this? Let Jenny handle it with Paul.

Every time he tried to walk away justifying the facts, Jack felt the pain of Guilt. Pain of social responsibility. If I ignore William today, tomorrow it can be me. He remembered the sorrowful face of his wife, who appeared for the police media appeal for witnesses. Police always uses victim's closest relative for media, as people generally do not come forward to assist police. He struggled a lot to justify and walk away. But he knew, he will not be able to sleep peacefully rest of his life because of overwhelming guilt.

Then Jack had only one choice. Go against the tide. He decided to say yes for the news article and get some advice from Jenny on how he should do this. But he did not know that was the most foolish decision he ever made.

10. The Research

At the midnight Jack send a message to Jenny "I will do the article." He thought Jenny will reply in the morning. But Jenny replied "Do not discuss in the office. We'll meet for lunch outside."

Jenny messaged Jack to meet at Hidden Lane. Jack arrived first, walked in found a small peaceful café, thought Jenny would like it. Jack send a message to Jenny. But Jenny told to meet at another place after fifteen minutes. Jack walked in to the cafe and found Jenny in a private lobby.

Jenny asked Jack to sit and was going through the menu.

She asked Jack "So you decided to die for William?"

Jack did not respond. Instead he said "how we can do this Jenny."

But Jenny did not ignore her first question. "You did not answer me Jack."

"Well, it's complicated. Whether I like it or not I have gone too far on this journey. Now I want to finish this. So I can die like a guiltless man if it is my fate."

Jenny waited until Jack ordered his lunch.

She continued. "We have to do a research on this Jack."

Jenny started how he should do this.

"First get all newspaper articles, social media news and police media reports on William's disappearance. Then go for the eye witnesses. Fortunately or unfortunately you are the first eye witness, since you met him at the English breakfast. Then you go to your friend John. If possible try to talk to the original eye witnesses. Also cross check whether their information is reliable. Record them as much as you can with their permission. Remember to build the trust with them. I will help you in between. You need to act fast since it is almost a week after his disappearance."

"Can I do all these at office without alarming Paul" Jack asked.

"No" Jenny told. "You can't do this at the office. You should have some private space for this. You can use this place for your office. This café belongs to one of my friends. There is a small room upstairs. He agreed to give it for free for a week. But for your safety, try not to go out unnecessarily. I will come and visit you time to time. I will tell Paul that you are on leave for a week on a private matter."

Jack nodded. "Thank you Jenny"

"OK then I need to leave for office now" Jenny got up. She introduced Jack to the owner and left the Café. Jack also left after few minutes later to bring his equipment back to his new office room.

Once Jack reached the Café with his laptop and equipment's, the owner gave a key to Jack. Café opens from 8.00 a.m. to 4.00 p.m. But Jack was given the freedom to use the room freely, as the owner lives next block of the Café.

Jack settled down quickly in the room and wrote down his tasks list for the research. The first the analysis of news articles on William. He used first Google advanced news research to find the last week news of William's disappearances. Surprisingly there were quite a lot of articles even after he minimized the research with most suitable key words. He tried alternative techniques and listed 44 news articles to research.

He went through all the articles. He could not find anything interesting, other than basic crime reporting of a disappearance. No one has mentioned of English Breakfast or Terry's office. Why these journalists have not gone that far? As per the articles William's disappearance was reported on Tuesday 9.00 a.m. William has arrived Glasgow in Sunday afternoon and checked – in to the Pipers, a 30 room guest house down the Byres Road. The manager of the hotel has reported to police. Jack decided to meet the manager. Secondly, he should go into Terry's office building. First he should investigate whether Terry is the only resident of the building as John explained. Then if necessary he should meet Terry.

Jack met the manager of the Pipers in the late evening same day. Hotel was a decent place to stay for business visits. It cannot be that expensive either. He waited almost 15 minutes to meet the manager in the small lobby. Jack walked into the manager, Steve's office room, introduced himself, and explained the reason for his visit.

Steve: Well Jack we actually informed everything to Police and I have seen this was reported in many newspapers during this week, but how can I help you anyway?

Jack: I went through all these news articles and identified that William's case has been under reported. That's why we are at the Jenny's Daily decided to go deeper to find more on this case. There may be other issues even crimes related to this single case Steve.

Steve: Well, I could not meet him at all, as he was here only for one night. But as per the information I received from my front office and room service staff, he was not a demanding or disturbing guest but a loner in his own world with his documents.

Jack: He was an estate broker.

Steve: Oh, I thought he must have been a researcher.

Jack: What happened to his belongings Steve?

Steve: Police took them away and they signed our log book for that. I got an acknowledgement letter as well later.

Jack: Any list of items given?

Steve: No, one baggage and few ordinary belongings, such as his pijama and undergarments and few items such as hair brush tooth brush etc., nothing much.

Jack: OK Steve, thank you very much for your time, good night.

Jack left the Hotel around 7.00 p.m. He decided to visit Terry's office next day morning and walked back to his apartment.

Next day morning he reached Terry's office building. John was not there at the steps as usual. Jack decided to walk in. It was a five storied old building. Walls have been neglected for sometimes. Off white walls look dirty with faded paint and cracks. Jack wandered why Terry selected this building for his office? How can he bring his customers here? He slowly walked up on the stair expecting somebody to be there on the first flow where Terry's office located. It was a dark green door. His name board was to the left of the main door. Jack knocked the door twice but no answer. He decided to go further up to find out any other residence in the building. He went up to second and third floor. There were four blocks on each floor. All green doors no names or numbers. He looked up at the stair case to find any evidence of residents. When he reached the fourth floor, he heard some voices in the apartment to his left. Couple of Male' voices. When he took a step forward, voices stopped suddenly. Jack thought of running down but decided to wait until anyone comes out.

He walked up to the door and knocked. He felt someone looking through the peep hole. After a few minutes a middle aged man opened the door. "Yes?" he asked.

"Well I came to meet Mr. Terry Blackstone, is he stay here? I knocked couple of time on his office door and seems nobody there." Jack explained.

"Why are you looking for him?" The man asked after scrutinizing Jack from top to bottom.

Jack thought why he just not give some information and let me go. He did not want to give much details to this stranger. "I am a journalist need to talk to him on some important matter."

"What's your name?" He asked rudely again.

"I am Jack this is my ID". He showed the ID to the stranger.

He waited for a while expecting something. Then he said "Sorry I can't help you. If he is not there, how he can open his office door? If I were you, would have given a call to him before come for the interview."

"May I have his telephone number please?" Jack asked again.

"Use a directory. He is a lawyer." And he closed the door rudely.

Jack was happy that he escaped without much damage done. Jack strongly believed that someone in the apartment was closely listening to their discussion.

He had a one more knock at Terry's office door. No body again.

Jack was relieved as he walked out of the building. He walked further down the road. But he wanted to observe the building from distance, without alarming anyone. He noted a restaurant opposite to the building. This could be an ideal place for spying. He quickly ran to the first floor and sat near a window that he can clearly see the entrance of Terry's office building. Jack ordered a coffee and a simple breakfast to buy time for his operation. This could be the longest breakfast he ever had in any Café in Glasgow. He did not have anything to admire in the breakfast but spent thirty five minutes to clean the plate, while half of the coffee yet remaining in the cup.

Jack finally saw some movements at entrance of the building. He was stunned with what he saw. It was no one else but Paul. Paul scanned both sides of the street and even looked at the restaurant. Jack hid his face partially behind the curtain to avoid Paul seeing him. After a while Paul slowly walked towards the city center.

First Jack thought he should follow Paul. But then he decided against it. He would get nothing just following him. Then he decided to pay the bill and leave the place. Before he pull out his wallet a gentlemen with dark suite sat in front him. A familiar face but he could not recall anything due to the sudden shock.

"What are you looking for Jack?" the gentlemen asked with a deep threatening voice. "I am Terry Blackstone, you questioned me at the community center right?"

Jack could not still recover from the shock. He spied on a suspect and the suspect conveniently walked up to him and now sitting in front of him. What an amateur detective and what a shame.

But Jack immediately adjusted to the situation. "Well....actually I came to meet you. I knocked on the door many times and no answer.

That's why I am waiting here desperately expecting you to come back to the office."

Obviously as per the features of his face, Terry did not believe Jack. But he asked, "Why are you desperately searching for me?"

Terry spread his hands either side of the table, looked straight into Jack's eyes. An intimidating strong vibe scanned through Jack's body, paralyzing him. But he recovered soon and asked his first question.

"Did William, who disappeared last Monday, visited you on that day morning?

Terry's face muscles relaxed and leaned back on the chair and folded his hands on his chest. But he never took his eyes away from Jack's eyes.

"Yes, he visited me." Terry answered. "I knew William before. Hope you know that he is an estate broker. I did some businesses with him in Manchester couple of years ago. Good guy, a true professional. He came to meet me for some advice on few properties here in Glasgow. I gave my advice on that. Then we walked out of my office. I had a meeting but he went off for his breakfast. I invited him for a dinner on the same day night which he accepted. But I did call him couple of time after 6.30 in the evening. He did not response. Then I thought he will call me later when he is free. But he didn't. Then I decided to meet him next day since he told me that he is leaving on Thursday. But next day morning I heard this shocking news. I immediately called police that I met him and all what happened in the morning. Then that afternoon I gave my statement to police." Then he paused for a while.

"Are you satisfied now Jack?" Terry asked again.

Jack was scribbling few notes on his note book.

"May I know the properties he was asking about here in Glasgow?"

Terry had a mockery smile on his face.

"It is confidential. I have given all that information to police. You can check with them." Terry concluded his discussion and stood up and pointed his index finger to Jack and told" Do not ever get into my property without my permission again. This is the first and the last warning. If you do that again I will inform police for trespassing." Then he turn back to Jack and walk toward the door. Before he left, he turned back and told Jack, "If you need anything call me and fixed an appointment." Then he left.

Jack watched Terry crossing the road and walking towards his office. He turned one more time and looked at the restaurant first floor window where Jack was seated. Then he disappeared into the building.

It took sometimes for Jack to realize that he was not frozen. He settled his bill and left for Hidden Lane. He had lot to discuss with Jenny. He wrote a draft article for newspaper. He summarized all bits and pieces of William's story in media, comparing Police media report. Then he included his own eye witness information and John's testimony. But he should have firsthand information on John's story. He should find him quickly and must meet his eyewitnesses soon.

Jenny arrived for lunch and Jack briefed his finding, which Jenny eagerly listened. He did not still discussed anything about Terry's office visit.

"Anything else Jack?" Jenny asked.

"Is it possible to get any information of the police investigation on William's disappearance, using your connections? Then we can interview those people concern as well." Jack explained.

"Yes can get, but we cannot write those in the newspaper. That may disturb police investigation, also it will be a threat for those witnesses, if an organized gang is involved in this case. So no point going on that lead Jack." Jenny was in his thoughts.

Jack informed "Then I will try to get John's statements confirmed."

Jenny agreed" Yes, that's good."

Jack did not informed anything happened with Terry and in his office building. Jack new that Jenny may not like him becoming a police detective. So he could not tell that he saw Paul coming out of the building.

But he just asked "Did Paul asked about me."

"Yes, I told you are on leave for a week on a personal matter." Jenny replied.

Jenny got up and about to leave his room. Then Jack remembered something that Jenny might be interested. "Jenny, I found one of William's face book photos shared saying that William had been seeing walking with a gentlemen near Klevingrove Park on Monday afternoon. This is contrasting John's statement that he went for English Breakfast for lunch and then disappeared.

Jenny stopped, closed the door, came back and sat on the chair again.

"Can you show me that Jack." Jenny asked Jack.

Jenny seems surprised or shocked but Jack could not figure it out clearly. Jack quickly searched the post and showed to Jenny. She checked carefully the photo and the background. Then she zoomed in for the faces. William's face is clear but can see only part of the face of the other gentlemen. Jack did not see that much in detail of this since it is a just a photo. He also not know exactly this photo was taken on that day or some other time.

The University Glasgow building in the background confirmed the photo was taken inside the Klevingrove Park. Date of the photo unknown but uploaded on last Tuesday. Then matters became worse for Jack.

11. The Photo

Jenny seems puzzled, unhappy or upset?

Jack interrupted "Will this photo help us to find some information on this?"

"Police did not tell anything on this" Jenny murmured. But Jack heard it. So she knows what police is doing on this case. Why she is not sharing this information with me? Jack thought. May be she is careful, to ensure that I do not use information in any irresponsible manner. He tried to justify Jenny's silence.

"I'll let you know. Send me the photo Jack, bye!" Jenny got up and left the room quickly.

Jack thought first he should cross check the reliability of John's statement. The possibility of that his statement on William may be extravagated with his experience in the street. After being homeless for years, John's mental health could have been deteriorated as well. If Jack could get the first witnesses interviewed, then he can think of second path for investigation based on the photo in the park.

Jack decided to stroll down in the city seeking for John. He walked down the University Road. Passed the concrete benches and walked into the Mall. He search through the Mall and went up to the stall where he met John. Nobody was there to inquire about John. He walked few rounds in the Mall and walked out back to the street. He checked in Byres Road, especially known for homeless, but John was not among them. Jack checked with few homeless people about John, but they did not know. Then Jack did not have any option, but wait for John.

Jack was very tired after a long walk in search of John. He decided to investigate further matters on the following day.

After dinner he was resting on his old couch. He thought of checking the face book post on William. But it was not available. It has been removed. Jack wandered why and how? Luckily he saved a screen shot of the post in his gallery. He checked the photo closely and then the post. Mr. William at the Klevingrove Park, 2.30 p.m.

Jack send a message to the member who posted the photo on the Facebook to meet for a discussion. He thought he will not get a reply. But within 15 minutes he got a message with a "yes". "When and where?" Jack replied. The reply was "today at 10.30 p.m. at Klevingrove Park entrance." Jack replied "Can we make it tomorrow morning?" Then he got the face book reply "I am leaving Glasgow tomorrow early morning. It might take couple of weeks before my return. Please confirm soon." Jack thought, is it safe to go there at this time? However, he had to take few daring decisions as he needs to get to the bottom of this crime. Jack replied, "Yes I will come." Then Jack got a positive response. Jack called Jenny to inform his meeting with Facebook member, but did not get any response. Jack left a message for her before leaving for Klevingrove Park. But he was unaware of his deadly fate.

12. The Abduction

Jack reach the park entrance by 10.15 p.m. He didn't see much crowd near the park. Jack was not that comfortable of this meeting place with a complete stranger. But he took this risk to make his investigation attractive for the newspaper, but only if this information is useful. He waited for long in the cold, tucking his both hands in the jacket pockets and walking back and forth to keep him warm. Few vehicles passed by. Five minutes already passed on scheduled time. Jack decided to leave by 10.45 back to his apartment.

Jack patiently waited until 10.45. Then he decided leave the place, blaming himself for following an unreliable lead. While he slowly started walking towards the apartment, a white car slowed down just behind him. He thought this could be the guy who messaged me. Then a stocky medium size man got out of the car. He was with a black face mask, which is not common these days. Jack thought maybe he was trying to hide his face for safety.

"Hi, are you waiting for someone for a Photo, ...William?" the stranger asked.

"Yes, I am." Jack replied.

"Sorry for the delay, I was bit busy, please get into the car, we'll have a chat in a pub nearby. The stranger apologies.

"No issue" Jack try to pacify him. "Sure we'll go." Jack got into the car, while the stranger got into the driving seat. He started and moved forward the car immediately, once Jack fastened his seatbelt. It took some time for Jack to realize there was another guy seated behind him in the car. But while he was thinking a wet handkerchief with a strong smell came from behind and blocked his nose and the mouth. Jack struggled to release from the grip but his eyes failed and numbness of the body spread quickly all over the body. He just fell into the darkness.

Jack got his senses back little later. He opened his eyes. He felt like he just woke up in the morning. He felt tired and bit dizzy. But he tried to stretch his hands and gain some strength back. But then he realized he cannot move his hands. Then he got back his senses fully and noted that he was tied on to a wooden chair. He was under a bright light. He can see clearly a distance of four feet radius. It seems to be an old basement. Floor is cracked in few places and many excess broken furniture stacked further behind of his chair. He could not see any further because of the darkness. The brightness of the light is too strong Jack could not look up much longer. He just had to wait for something to happen.

Then he heard some footsteps in front of him. A man walked up to him but did not come closer to him. He pulled a chair and sat in front of him. He did not talk. Jack was waiting for him to talk. But it was dead silent for a while. Then Jack lost his patient.

"What do you want from me?" Jack asked angrily.

Then he pulled his chair little closer so that Jack can see his face. Now he is at the edge of four feet radius circle. It was a familiar face.

He was dressed with the full suite, tie and well-polished black shoes. He was leaned back and folding his hands around his chest. His closed right palm lifted up to his mouth while he was gazing at Jack. Jack noted a signet ring on his pinky finger on his lifted hand. There was a blue and black art work in the center of the ring.

"Jack....Jack....Jack." The man uttered slowly.

Then he continued in the same tone "Jack I told you before to help us to get the information that you have. But you did not do that. Now you are creating too many problems for us. You should have given the documents and stay away from this for good."

Then Jack remembered the man's face. This is the guy who came to meet him to his office asking for documents and evidence to act against Terry, representing a rival gang fighting against Bodyguards.

"You told you need to work against Terry, the Bodyguards."

He started laughing loudly. The echo of the room was so horrible. His laughter echoed in the room. Also the sound confirmed that was a basement, no openings what so ever.

It took some time for him to calm down. Finally he became so calm. Silence was so frightening. Jack was extremely frighten, His clothes are wet with sweat. But he did not show his fear to his opponent.

Finally he spoke. "You know Jack, you as a journalist, observes a system not a society. A system run by a few powerful people. We can call them an Elite. The Elite runs everything that you see, even they are not visible. We are the wheels of that system. The Elite oil them and maintain them to ensure that the system runs smoothly. You journalists are the wheel blockers. That is why you are here."

Jack was confused, and asked "what did I do to you guys?"

The basement become very silent again. Meantime, since Jack's eyes are adjusted to low lights beyond, he scanned the basement carefully slowly. Then he saw another two people standing little further in the room. Once seems to be woman and the other a man. Jack thought they are planning something very dangerous.

"Mr. William became too nosy for our businesses. He tried to become a wheel blocker like you. Then he had to go. He was seated on this same chair few days ago. He started like you, strong and fearless. Then he realized his actual fate to be. He beg for his life desperately. We have to execute him, the orders from the Top."

Jack thought it is the end of his life, but determine to keep fighting until the last minute, he asked "Why did you kill him?"

"You can ask him when you meet him there." He smiled and got up.

The man came close to Jack. Then he started walking circles around Jack. After third round he took an injection out of his top pocket of his coat vest, he started walking around again playing with the injection in his hand.

"William was asking unnecessary questions about a property belongs to one of our seniors. It is not his business. It could have been belongs to someone else, may be legally. But now it is ours. He knew too much information about the property. He was trying to get the property back to the original owner. He cannot do that in this system. He learned it in a painful manner." The man spoke softly at the beginning, later his voice increased words spit out quickly.

Then he stopped suddenly at Jack's left. By this time Jack was so tired with his fear. He was bowing his head down and waiting for his punishment. It was a moment that fear becomes useless. His emotions became numb. He abandoned his hope of life and tried to recall what good he has done in this world.

Then the man's thundering voice blasted into his ears, "AND NOW YOU ARE CHALLENGING US JACK??? NOW GET THIS AND FEEL HOW WE FEEL.

Something pricked left side of his neck, it was like drilling his neck and whole of his body danced with the shock, he screamed with all his strength as long as he can. Then suddenly whole basement became silent. Jack fell back in to an endless darkness.

Jack opened his eyes slowly. First he thought he got up from his bed in the morning. But he was dressed. His whole body was numb. He tried to lift his head slowly and then he realized he was sleeping in his office on his table. His keys and wallet spread on the table. It was early morning 4.30 a.m. He straighten his body and leaned against the chair. The light near his table was on. He did not felt cold. Then he noted the heater also was on.

The person who brought Jack to his office knew the office keys, access codes, and the exactly where Jack sits. Is it possible the same guy who came to meet Jack and then later kidnapped him. But how he know all these information. He just spend very short time in the meeting room.

Jack slowly stood up and walked few steps forward he felt very tired. He walked up to the coffee machine. He pulled a chair near the coffee machine as he did not have strength to stand even for a while. He drank a coffee and gained strength to stand up. Jack decide go home and rest while he has some strength in the body. He left the office by 6.00 a.m., got into a taxi and left for his apartment.

13.Freedom

Jack had a homemade breakfast and fell on to his bed with the dress on. He did not wake up until noon. He felt better and immediately had a shower. He sank into his couch and reflected the events of the previous night. He was trying to fix the jigsaw puzzle piece by piece. Jack's biggest confusion was whether Terry and the gangster he met yesterday are in the same side or opponents? Who is the woman and the man in the darkness?

Then Jack's mobile vibrated. It was Jenny. She was at the Hidden Lane office room waiting for Jack. Jack explained his long story in the shortest possible way so that she can experience the frightening night. But Jenny was not that enthusiastic. He thought that's because the unwanted risk that he took.

"Now what are you going to do Jack?" Jenny asks plainly. "Are you going to police on this?"

"I do not know the people who kidnapped me?" Jack said.

"People? Were there any others? Did you see them?" Jenny inquired.

"Not really, but there was a woman and a man in the basement in the dark." Jack replied.

"Are you sure you didn't see them?" Jenny tried to get a confirmation.

Jack was puzzled. But again Jenny tried to reduce the tone of the question by asking "No I just wanted to know, if you saw them, you can inform police with some identification right?"

"But the best evidence is our office CCTV camera images. Can we get that for me Jenny?" Jack inquired.

Jenny paused for a while "Ok, then come to office this evening. I'll try to retrieve them for you."

"Thank you Jenny "Jack got up to dress for office.

Jack reached office by 3.30 in the evening. Paul was at his table, but he was not that friendly as he used to be. He nodded his head and was glued to his laptop. Jack slowly walked up to Jenny's room. She was on a call but told him to come in.

Jenny finished the call and look at Jack in a strange manner.

"What dates and times Jack?" Jenny asked while she is scrolling down in his laptop.

"Early this morning, around 4.30 and last Wednesday 2.00 p.m. onwards" Jack answered.

She took couple of minutes to retrieve what Jack needed. But then she looked at Jack surprisingly. "I don't see anything Jack" Jenny told. She turned the laptop to Jack and showed him.

"This was last Wednesday." Jenny explained. "See, here you are seated at your table, and this is meeting room. Nobody. Scroll down further nobody. Then again see this morning. Nobody in the office. Nobody on you table and no one has entered as well." Jenny concluded.

Jack felt helpless also fear grew in his mind. Am I gone mad?

"I don't know what to say Jenny" Jack broke the long silence in the room.

"I think you need a good rest Jack. That is what you should do. Why don't you go back to your home town for week and come back later Jack?" Jenny suggested.

Jack didn't say anything but thanked Jenny and got up and left for his table. Then he noticed that Jenny also having a similar ring of the gangster who tortured him. With blue and black artwork in the middle. Why Jack didn't noticed this ring all these days? Jack came back to his table took his note book from his drawer and decided leave to his apartment again.

"Are you on leave Jack, Jenny told me?" Paul asked without taking his eyes off from his laptop.

Jack tried to check what he is doing. He was typing something speedily. Then Jack noticed the ring on his finger. The same ring with blue and black artwork. Jack got up and walked towards the door. Then Paul looked at him. "Is she?" Jack asked and left the office.

Jack came back home as a helpless and broken man. Jack was shocked what he saw and tried to fix the puzzle as he felt right. If they, the gangster at the basement, Jenny and Paul all having the same ring, it cannot be a coincidence. Even if the ring is a traditional Scottish ring, it is not possible all three people having same taste or interest of Scottish culture. If the ring is a symbol of an organization, then Jenny and Paul are also in the same group. Terry told that he knows of Paul before. And Jack saw Paul was walking out of Terry's office building. Paul and Terry meetings cannot be interviews. There should be something more for that relationship. So it is possible that Terry also in the same group. Jack was finally found a hypothesis to work on. But questions was, are they Bodyguards?

All our societies have perfectly veiled system run by most powerful people. They are motivated with power, money and lust but not on human values. Their pride motivate them to crush the ordinary and walled up them with fear. The fear wall remains until the apocalyptic will occur, where the hidden secrets unveiled. Jack, you and me have to fight against the wall of fear and the systems, to avoid to become salves of the secret systems. The freedom has a price. It can be a life or unimaginable destruction. But there is no option but every individual has to fight for this freedom. Jack's imaginary puzzled completed with a positive and joyful note. He thought to become a freelance investigative journalist. With that Jack decided not to go back to his job but to do his job as a freelance journalist against the "System".

14. The First project

The first project of Jack, as an investigative journalist was obviously William. But to survive as an amateur freelance journalist in the city is not that easy. So he needed to do few part-time jobs to cover his expenses. Next day, Jack checked online for part-time vacancies, noted down few and was in the city center shortly, seeking for jobs. Jack got an offer as a sales assistant in a mall before noon. 20hrs per week, 9.66 pounds per hour. That was sufficient to cover his rent. He thought of doing another job during the weekend to cover his other expenses.

Jack saw John with another middle aged man, while he was just opening the gate for his apartment building. They were walking toward him. They did not see Jack until he called them. Jack was so happy to see John as he needed for his first project badly. Then John introduced other, "Jack this is Gavin, a former detective, now private investigator and lawyer too. We were discussing about your uncle William as well." Jack was so happy to hear that and invited them to his small apartment for a coffee.

Gavin was a tall man, with a physique of an athlete. He was silent but observant. Seems to be a good listener. He scanned Jack's apartment carefully. Jack was so embarrassed of his messy apartment. But Gavin seems to be satisfied with his final conclusion.

After long discussion Gavin broke his silence.

"The biggest mistake you did Jack was opening the investigation at the wrong place and the people. You should have avoided all this mess if you contacted a professional investigator."

"As you noted at the day one, possible reason for William's death, I believe, is the documents you saw he was pulling from the briefcase. If you got those, the rest would have been so easy."

"There is someone, who does not like that William had these documents in his hand. If you got the documents then we know the person who got annoyed."

This is interesting, Jack thought. "But how we get these documents to our hand?" Jack asked Gavin.

He said, "As William was an estate broker, I guess this is something to do with a property. I need to get some information, how a person like William get these documents. I need to investigate on his practice. Then the rest I can get from Land Register of Scotland. Leave it to me. I will get these documents for you."

Jack was so glad to hear this from Gavin.

John interrupted, "So Jack thank you for coffee, we have to leave now. But don't worry Gavin will do what he promised for you."

"John is my good friend, don't worry about the cost. I can handle it. I heard this story from John and was shocked. We'll team up for the Justice. Justice is the remuneration we should look forward to. See you Jack."

Jack watched them moving out with a great satisfaction.

Gavin did not waste much time on the case. He got his contacts in Manchester to re-create William's character in his office. Once he studied William and his dealings, he noted the properties he was interested, property values and customers he was dealing with. According to his characteristics, Gavin listed ten similar properties in Glasgow.

He did not stop at that point. He got all these deed copies with owner ship transfers for last ten years. He dropped three properties from the list. The information revealed these properties are most unlikely available for sale. Rest was a puzzle. But there was one deed that was interesting. It was Terry's office building.

Gavin met Jack after two weeks in a cafe down Ashton lane. He gave a lengthy explanation of his investigation. Jack was busy noting down points. Jack had so many questions for Gavin. However the progress was good. But the way ahead was not clear. How they connect theses remaining properties to William, so they could present these finding for a court case.

While they were pondering Gavin presented the shocking document to Jack. That was Terry's office building deed and ownership transfer documents.

Gavin explained the ownership transfers and present owners of the building. There were two joint owners they were Jenny Campbell and Paul Moray.

"What? I can't believe this Gavin" Jack exclaimed.

Gavin was surprised. "What you can't believe?"

"I was working with Jenny and Paul, at Jenny's daily almost over a year. I never knew they own a building together in Glasgow. They are not married as per my understanding. How they own this property jointly?"

Gavin said "I think we have a clue here. Leave it to me I'll get how and why?"

Jack said "I will come with you wherever you go to find this information. I would like to see how truth is revealing first time and it's exciting."

Gavin thought Jack is acting like a child. But he let him join. They searched Scottish people and Scottish indexes. They found some confusing information.

Gavin and Jack decided to go to National Library. Gavin had a friend who is an expert of family histories in Scotland. Within twenty minutes both of them were sitting in front of a sixty year old gentlemen, who seems exactly matching with surrounded very old books, files and documents.

George, Gavin's old friend, looked through his rounded lenses at both Gavin and Jack.

"Jenny Campbell you said?"

"Campbell's were great Scottish landowners for centuries. She could be related to one of them I believe."

"Then Paul, yeah Morays also same. But we need to find the connection. It is unlikely these landowners related as a result of a marriage. Yeah...but we'll find out the story behind them. Give me couple of days Gavin"

Gavin and Jack left the building leaving the rest of the research to Gavin's old friend in the National Library. Jack was not happy to leave without information. He left the library as a small child who had to leave his favorite toy behind. Gavin noticed his sorrowful face.

"What's wrong Jack?" Gavin asked.

"I wanted some information now. Not couple of days later. It is frustrating."

Gavin started laughing "Jack, you act like a child. This immaturity lead you to all those troubles that you face now. But now you should know, it takes time to generate reliable evidence. Those evidence could be very strong so we can build the case only with what we are going to get from the Library."

Jack satisfied with Gavin's explanation, and decided not to act in such a manner which might disturbed Gavin's hard work.

15. The Family

George informed Gavin and Jack to meet him one afternoon in a café down Ashton Lane. Jack was impatient, but remembered Gavin's advice, controlled his restless emotions. Gavin was silent. George sipped his bear couple of times. He was talking about their friendship and fun they had together. Jack felt that his losing his patients but bottled up as a respect for Gavin.

Finally George spoke what it mostly matters to them

"This story was really interesting Gavin. I never heard something like this before."

"That's interesting" Gavin was listening carefully.

"Eadmund Campbell married Anne Hunter and lost all his inheritance, properties and wealth, as his parents did not agree with Anne Hunter as their son's wife. Anne was from an ordinary farming family in Yorkshire. Eadmund was not worried, moved to Glasgow and was working as an accountant. He bought a house down West End raised Jenny their only daughter. Anne owned the house by Edmund's last will after his death after a shot illness. "

"He had only a house, in Glasgow?" Jack was surprised.

"Yes he did not save much"

"But Anne married to Malcom Moray a medium scale property owner after Eadmund's death. Anne could have been pretty woman to be attracted by men from rich families. I cannot justify her relationships otherwise. Malcom had two sons. Paul was the eldest. His brother was Colin. Did you know about Colin Jack?"

"I haven't heard of him. Paul never mentioned about his family"

"I think I know him. " Gavin interrupted. "He is a broker and known as a notorious character in Glasgow."

"You are right Gavin." George agreed. "He controls part of West End underground as per my knowledge."

"Are they the Bodyguards?" Jack asked.

"No. Bodyguards are well organized criminal gang in Britain. Colin had a small city gang."

"Ok now let me complete the story" George interrupted.

"Malcom was gambler. He sold most of properties and wealth for gambling. But he had one building remaining down the University Avenue. That was again given to Anne after his death. I am not sure how they share these properties among their children because Anne also died few years ago."

"Wow what a story. Now we know something to move on Gavin" Jack expressed his relief.

George gave the documents of the family tree with full names and relationships before left the café after a good meal.

But Gavin and Jack had work to do.

Gavin said "we need to get some information on Colin, Jack. We are blind about him. Is he owns their house or they have some other properties as well?"

"I like to see his photo. I know Jenny and Paul but not Colin."

"Oh I can show him" Gavin opened his mobile and browsed on the Facebook.

"Here this is Colin" Gavin showed a photo of Colin.

Jack felt faintish once he saw the photo. That was the guy who tortured him in the basement.

"Gavin, this is the guy who attacked me in the basement. I have no doubt this is him."

"Oh we have a clue then Jack. This is a good beginning. Let me get other information of their properties. Then we can move on with this crystal clear story. We are almost done Jack" Gavin seems very happy.

Gavin reached his friends in Land registry of Scotland. He spend a week on this investigation and at the end he got all documents ready for their case. He met Jack at his apartment one late evening.

Gavin explained the story of the family to Jack with the information and documents he obtained from his friends in Land registry.

"The Terry's office building name is 'Schoolhouse'. This was used as a university staff quarters roughly 50 or more years ago. This was sold late to private property owners and used mainly for public accommodation purposes. Malcom Moray was the last owner of the property before Jenny and Paul. Their main house which was owned by Eadmund Campbell, currently owned by Colin. But both this property ownerships should have been transferred to Anne. But her name was not in title records anywhere. Ownerships were mysteriously directly transferred to Jenny, Paul and Colin."

Jack was listening eagerly but interrupted for a while.

"Gavin, ownership transfer is not what we are focusing on. Why they abducted me and who murdered William and why?"

"This is what exactly I'm trying to explain Jack." Gavin continued his explanation.

"Why they abducted you? They did not want you to find, how William disappeared. Why? They are involved in that incident. If so, why they did not like William? Because he knew some information they did not want to reveal. This could be the ownership of the Schoolhouse building."

"William was an experience estate broker. His customers were reputed people. He would never let his clients to buy a property with vague ownership. Because he would not risk his hard earned reputation as an estate broker."

"The ownership of the building is exactly what we have to find out. That is the case we have to file. Then all other cases will fit in so easily"

Jack and Gavin concluded. They decided to walk in the most dangerous road of all. The secrets in lost Last wills of Eadmund Campbell and Malcom Moray needed to be revealed.

Jack was the only one who experienced the danger of finding the truth of William. Jack wanted to justify their decision.

Jack questioned Gavin, "Aren't they Bodyguards? They can kill us so easily right?"

"When I got to know about your story and the Bodyguards from John, I knew they are not Bodyguards." Gavin talk about Bodyguards first time with Jack. "They have their own businesses in Glasgow. They do not do contract killings. But they do kill their opponents who compete with their businesses. Colin just borrowed their name to threaten you. But they are not bodyguards. John knew some of the brutal murders of Bodyguards. But rest of the story that interpreted by John could be just a fairy tale in his imagination. I don't think Bodyguards ever followed you. Colin's gangsters must have followed you to frighten you."

"We have to protect only form Colin then?" Jack asked Gavin.

"Jack you don't worry. I will handle it carefully. I will give an update periodically. Then we will decide how to proceed from there."

Gavin left Jack's apartment almost close to midnight.

16. The Lost last will

Gavin visited National Library next day morning. He sat in front of George and was silent until his friend finished his documentation work in the library. George handled the archives, documents only available for research purposes. He is responsible for protection of those old documents and books as well.

Gavin kept a small envelop on the table. George looked at him instantly.

"Just some pocket money for you George"

"I did not expect any money from you just a piece of information."

"Then you consider this as an advance payment, for a big job."

"Now what?" George asked.

"I need copies of Eadmund Campbell's and Malcom Moray's original last wills. Can you do that for me?"

"That's a serious request Gavin. Highly confidential information. Yes I can get it for you but why I have to undermine my moral values?"

"One man was murdered. Another being under dead threats. If you give this to me, I can nail the criminals behind these crimes. But up to you George. But let me know."

Gavin left George leaving envelop of cash for him. He was thinking for a plan B if George decides not to provide the documents.

After sometime, Jack was in an old Ashton Lane café. Not English Breakfast but another peaceful location in the lane. He was enjoying a coffee in the morning, relaxing, with partly closed eyes. But it was not for long. A gentlemen came and sat in front of him. A short, stout man with messy overgrown hair with the beard. Jack first thought he just wanted sit there, but was wandering as the café is almost empty at that time. He looked restless and had an envelope in his hand. Jack thought he needed some help.

"Sir are you all right? You need any help?" Jack asked the gentlemen.

He did not response but slowly pushed the documents to Jack.

Jack looked at him. He thought he is a dumb beggar requesting him to read his story. Jack always prefer to help others whenever he can. He kept his hand over the envelope and then dumb beggar spoke.

"Open. You need these documents"

Jack opened and pulled out the bundle of documents. He found couple of title deeds and a title investigation report in it. He looked at the man seated in front of him surprisingly.

"Read" he said pointing the documents. There were too titles deeds.

Jack check carefully. One was Anne Moray to Evan Smith and other one was from Anne to Jenny Campbell and Paul Moray.

Then he checked the title investigation report. In that Malcom Moray to Anne and to Evan Smiths transfers had been not recorded but only Malcom Moray to Jenny and Paul was recorded in the land registry.

Jack lifted his head and asked "Who was Evan Smith?"

But there was no one seated in front of him. The man disappeared. Jack ran out of the café. He was searching for the old gentlemen but could not find him anywhere.

He came back and check the documents one more time carefully. Yes, two ownership transfers in between was not recorded. Jenny's and Paul's owner ship of the building could be a fraud as Anne and Evan Smith ownership was missing.

Jack called Gavin to inform what he got from the stranger. He came to meet shocked and puzzled Jack, who was glued to set of documents.

"This is shocking Gavin." Jack spoke before Gavin.

"A stranger came and sat in front of me gave these documents and then disappeared."

"A Ghost Jack?"

"No I saw him walking down the street but disappeared in the crowd. But these documents are real. Can we get these confirmed by the Land Registry?"

"Yes we can Jack, let me do that. I will try to find further documents such as last wills of Eadmund Campbell and Malcom Moray. Then our case is close. We will find a clue on William as well."

"Great, we need a trusted lawyer to put all these evidence together to file a case against Jenny and Paul."

Gavin did not waste a second. He got the documents from Jack and walked swiftly down the Ashton Lane. But Jack felt very uncomfortable and stressed. He turned to Byres road and had a slow walk towards to his apartment. He did not lift his head but his mind was flying in many directions. He just wanted to erase all in his mind. He wish his mind to be a computer drive. Then he could reformat his mind to start fresh. But it was not that easy.

While he was breathing fresh cold air, just looked at the crowded side walk in front of him. He wanted to cross the road and avoid the crowd. While he was just about to cross he saw a man begging in front of a souvenir shop. Man with overgrown hair and beard. Face was familiar. He changed his mind and slowly walked towards him.

He gave a pound note to him. He was surprised and looked at Jack. Yes, it is him. The stranger who gave the documents to Jack.

"Shall we have some coffee, together?"

He scratched his forehead, not knowing what to say.

"Yes." He said finally.

Jack and the stranger walk up to a café, bought coffee and started walking down the street.

"What's your name?" Jack asked first.

"You are the one who gave me the documents in Ashton lane café right?"

"Yes...... I am." He replied softly.

"I got it from a stranger, but I did not meet him again. My name is Evan Smith. I was an owner of few properties. But my family cheated me and left nothing for me. But I managed to file a case. I got considerable compensation. I bought the Schoolhouse down University Avenue with that money. Rest I lost for gambling. But I received rent from the building which I spend on unsuccessful businesses and got into debt. Then I wanted to sell the property to pay my debts."

"Then you sold it?" Jack interrupted.

"No, I told Terry, a lawyer who was on rent in the building, my intention to sell the property. He said can sell but he needs all original documents. I gave all to him. Then days passed by. Nothing happened. I asked Terry to return the documents but he did not. I was in a serious debt issue. All my creditors started troubling me daily. I beg Terry to help me. He agreed to give a loan to pay my debts but in return I have to give all rent income to him. I was desperate. I agreed to sign a document. I got rid of my debts and also the property I owned. Now Terry says building was not belong to me but to the daughter and the son of the previous owner. He said I cheated him. But I know I pay money to previous lady owner. But I did not register this transfer. I was so foolish."

"Now where do you stay?" Jack asked.

"No place. Terry chased me from the building saying that I cheated him."

"How do you know I needed this documents?"

"I met John one day some time ago in front of Schoolhouse. He showed you and told 'if you know any information of this building you can share with him, he is a journalist.'"

"I did not tell John anything of these documents. But I was searching for you desperately to handover these documents. But I did not see you until I met you in the café."

"Thank you Evan for your effort. This is a great help for justice. Do you know one guy was killed because of this property?"

"Who was that?" Evan asked eagerly.

"He was William Selwyn."

"No. He did not die, Jack."

"What, how do you know?" Jack was desperate.

"He came to meet me after this incident. But he told me, he was abducted tortured and threaten by Terry and the new owners of the building."

"He was lucky to escape them. But was disguised and hiding since then. I met him one day in a small ally. But did not talk much. He gave these documents for me to get back the property. But I do not have money to do that. That's why I gave it to you Jack."

"Thank you Evan. This was a great news and a great help for me. I will do my best to bring justice for you and William."

Jack got a call from Gavin.

"Jack, all done. I got the documents. Found a good lawyer. Don't worry about his fees. He will do it free for me. We may have to pay government expenses only."

"That is amazing Gavin. Well Gavin do you have a weak heart?"

"Why, what's the matter Jack?"

"I have a big surprise for you."

"What?"

"Gavin, I met Evan Smith. I am with him now. William also not dead. He is alive in the city. So we have all witnesses we wanted. We just need to protect them"

"Wow, I can't believe this Jack. Oh... unbelievable. Don't worry about their security. I am a security consultant as well. I will protect them. We must celebrate Jack. So your first project is almost over Jack."

"Yes Gavin, not without your great help. We'll meet up soon Gavin. Bye for now."

"All done Evan. You don't worry. It's all done."

Jack put his hand over Evan's shoulder and walk joyfully down the road. He could not explain how happy he is. Was it because William is living, or he found Jenny and Paul's true identity, or he just about to accomplish his first tasks as a freelance journalist. May be because he was able to contribute for justice for all who needed most. But he did not know exactly the reason. But he was happy. Very happy. He saw the whole world around him so beautiful, and as the best place to live forever, after a very long time.

- THE END -

| Page

Don't miss out!

Visit the website below and you can sign up to receive emails whenever SUSANTHA FERNANDO publishes a new book. There's no charge and no obligation.

https://books2read.com/r/B-A-CXOX-NSDHC

BOOKS 2 READ

Connecting independent readers to independent writers.